Contents

Characters

Jake   He's interested in martial arts and wants to become a modern day ninja!

Dan   He likes everyone to know how fit he is. Jake and Dan think that girls and martial arts don't mix.

Ethan   He likes sport but not as much as his friends. He has a sister so is used to girls.

Mia   She thinks that a fit brain is as important as a fit body.

 **Holly**   She wants to try martial arts but is afraid of getting hurt.

Narrator   The narrator tells the story.

What's on the flyer?

Narrator	It's the summer holidays. Jake, Dan and Ethan are bored.
Jake	What do you want to do?
Dan	I dunno. What do you want to do?
Ethan	Go to the arcade?
Jake	Nah, too many kids hang out there.
Dan	We could go and see a movie.
Jake	Yeah. Got any money?
Dan	No. You?

Ethan   Not enough.

Dan   We could go to your place?

Ethan   Can't, my sister had a sleepover.
There are girls everywhere.

Dan   Cool.

Jake   Definitely not cool.
His sister's eight.

Narrator   They walk into town and hope
something will turn up.

Ethan   The sports centre's over there.
Let's check it out.

Jake   Why? It'll only have holiday stuff
for kids.

Ethan   I wanted to do junior gym
when I was little. But Mum
never took me.

Dan   Something's up.
A bunch of guys just went in.

Ethan   She took my sister
to junior gym though.

Jake   Your mum must love her
more than you.

Narrator   They see a flyer pinned on the notice
board. Dan snatches it off the board
although two girls are reading it.

Dan   Hey, this is all right.
Listen up.

Mia   Don't mind us, will you?

Dan   Okay.

Holly   It's not like we were reading it
or anything.

Dan   Good.

Narrator Dan holds the flyer. Ethan and Jake
read aloud over his shoulder.

Ethan "Want to try martial arts?
Don't know where to start?
Try us!"

Jake "Learn to defend yourself in four days."

Mia Gee, they're good.
Do you think they can read
joined up writing?

Holly No, but they don't have to.
See, there are drawings too.

Narrator Dan hands the flyer to Mia.

Dan Nothing here to interest you.
Apart from me, that is.

Jake What do you think, Ethan?

Ethan I think it's because I broke my ankle
being Superman.

Jake   What?

Ethan   Why Mum never took me to junior gym.

Jake   I meant about this.
Do we give it a try?

Ethan   Sure.

Dan   Count me in.

Narrator Inside, a group of teens stand
with an instructor.
The boys check them out.

Jake   I can't see any of those guys
being any good. Can you?

Dan   No way. I could take them all on
blindfolded and win.

Ethan   Not those two.

Jake   They're the instructors, you loser.

Dan   Oh great, look who it is.

Narrator The girls from outside are walking over to join them.

Jake What are you doing here?

Mia What does it look like?

Holly We're going to do martial arts.

Ethan Can girls do that?

Dan We don't want you hanging out with us.

Holly Believe me, we don't want to
hang around with you.

Mia It isn't up to us anyway.
The instructor told us to wait here.

Holly The other group's full.
He's seeing if he has enough of us
for a second group.

Mia I hope he has. I so want to learn
how to balance my body and mind.

Holly Me too – and learn about inner peace.

Jake You're kidding, right?

Mia   No. That's why people do martial arts.

Holly   What are you here for?

Dan   To fight, of course.

Jake   Same.

Ethan   And it's free.

Narrator The instructor comes over.
He writes down their names
and tells them they'll be the
second group.

Dan   I'm out of here.

Jake   Yeah, let's go. I'm not being in a group
with those two.

Narrator Inside the hall there's loads of action.
People are doing judo, tae kwon do,
boxing and kick-boxing.

Ethan   Check out the demo first.

Mia   There are girls there too.
            Look, three of them.

Dan   The guys are good.
            They move fast.

Ethan   I count four girls. It's hard to tell
            sometimes.

Jake   I've changed my mind. I'll stay.
            Ninjas must know all the martial arts.

Narrator The instructor gives them a form
             to take home. He tells them to meet
             back at the hall the next day
             at nine and to wear loose clothes.

Dan   Okay. I'll come too.
            But I'm not happy.

Mia   Afraid we're going to show you up?

Dan   As if.

Scene 2
The obstacle course

Narrator The next day, the hall looks different.
One side has foam shapes set up
as an obstacle course. The other side
has punch bags.

Dan Hey, Ethan. It looks like you'll get to do
junior gym after all.

Ethan Yeah, it does, doesn't it?

Jake I don't want to do gym work.
I'm here for the martial arts.

Holly It's to test how fit we are.

Mia And see if we have good balance.

Jake   I don't care about balance –
when do we start fighting?

Ethan   Ninjas needed good balance, mate.
How else did they jump up high
and run along roofs and walls?

Narrator   The instructor shows them what to do
at each station of the obstacle course.

Dan   So we do what? Run across
on bits of foam?

Jake   Looks like it.

Ethan   Yay! It *is* junior gym.

Mia   No! That's not what the instructor said.
He said to jump and roll.

Holly   And think about your balance
at each station.

Scene 2   The obstacle course

Narrator Dan starts out on the obstacle course.
He plans to show off and make
the girls look useless.

Dan   One handspring coming up.
How good am I, guys?

Jake   Nah, you're running like a girl.
I'll show you how to do it ninja style.

Narrator Jake does a shoulder roll onto
the first bit of foam.

Jake   See? A ninja roll – low, small and tight.

Ethan   Watch this. A forward roll –
junior gym style.

Mia   Do you think we'll pick up any tips
from these guys?

Holly   On what not to do? Yeah!
Let's show them how it's done.

Narrator And they do. Then they all finish up
and go to the other side of the hall.
They are given boxing gloves,
headgear and a mouthpiece.

Holly Are we doing boxing?

Jake Nah, looks like tap-dancing to me.

Ethan Mum took my sister to tap classes.

Mia I think we do a mix
of martial arts stuff, Holly.

Holly This headgear's pulling on my hair.
It hurts.

Narrator Dan nudges his friends to play along.

Dan You think that hurts?
Wait until you box.

Holly I don't want to get punched.

Jake You'll get the hang of not getting hurt.

Dan   After you've been punched a few times.

Mia   Don't listen to them. The instructor
             won't let anyone get hurt.
             He'll show us how to hold up our
             hands to block the punches.

Narrator Jake punches his gloves together.

Jake   You won't know what hit you.

Dan   Yes they will. It'll be us!

Holly   Don't talk about us as if we're not here.

Dan   Hey, can you hear a voice?

Jake   No.

Ethan   Yes! It's Holly.

Narrator Holly and Mia punch their gloves together.

Mia We can hit back, you know.

Ethan Well you've got me scared.

Dan Boxing is great.

Mia What's great about it?

Dan Two people beat each other up. What's not great?

Narrator The girls talk with the instructor. They report back to the boys.

Holly The instructor said that boxing isn't about beating people up.

Dan Did he? That's weird. What's it about then?

Holly He said it's good for hand and eye skills.

Mia And it makes your mind and body fit.

Narrator They go up to the punchbags.
Mia taps the big body-shaped bag.

Mia This is really heavy.
It's hard to move.

Jake Not for me it isn't.
Punching like this makes you strong.

Holly What's with this basketball
stuck on a stick?

Ethan You punch it quickly, like this.
It builds up your hand speed.

Narrator The rest of the day is spent learning to box. Afterwards the boys head off.

Dan Today was great.
Hey, I've got a good way
to keep the girls freaked.

Narrator He shouts out to the girls
as they head out.

Dan It should be fun to spar with you.

Mia What?

Dan I asked the instructor.
He said we'll have time
if we come early tomorrow.

Scene 3
Jazz boxing

Narrator The next day, the boys meet up
outside. When they enter,
they stare in surprise.

Holly You're late.
We thought you'd chickened out.

Mia Don't look so shocked, Dan.
This was your idea.

Narrator The instructor helps everyone
with the gear.

Dan Did you watch them spar yesterday?

Ethan A bit. Their punches didn't
move the bag.

Dan So we're going to thrash them?

Jake Yeah, we're fast and strong.

Mia They're doing it again.
Talking like we're not here.

Holly They don't get it, do they?
It's important to be clever,
not just fast and strong.

Mia Yep. Good boxers use their brains
as well as their fists.

Dan Hey, I'm cool. You use your brain.
I'll stick with my fists.

Narrator   The teams spar – Holly against Dan
and Mia against Jake.
The instructor teaches Ethan
how to referee.

Jake   What are you doing?

Mia   Ducking and weaving.

Jake   Stop doing it!
I can't tell where you'll be next.

Mia   That's the point.

Jake   No it's not. I throw punches at you
as fast as I can and you block them.

Dan   Holly's the same. She's swaying
like a cobra before … Ow! … it attacks.

Ethan   Awesome footwork, Holly.
It's really fast. Yours too, Mia.

Holly   We've done jazz ballet.

Ethan   I thought so.
My sister does jazz ballet too.

Dan   Stay still, will you?
I haven't landed one punch.

Narrator Their time is up. The instructor helps
them take off the gear.

Holly   That was fantastic. Boxing rocks.

Mia   I thought only men could do it.
But thanks to Dan, I know girls
can box too.

Holly   And do it better.

Narrator The boys help get the exercise mats
out of the storeroom.

Jake   Great plan, Dan.
They look really freaked.

Dan   How was I to know they'd dance
instead of punch?

Ethan   They're girls, aren't they?

Narrator   They start up a bad song as they drag
the mats across the floor.

Dan   What – will – make them go?

Jake   Me be-ing agg – ro?

Dan   Me be-ing mach – o?

Ethan   Us do-ing tae kwon – do.

Jake   Yeah, it's really physical.
They'll hate it.

Narrator The girls join them for the first exercise. The instructor swings a padded bat, first at their head and then at their feet.

Mia Tuck your body under and roll.

Holly And watch him before, during and after the roll.

Ethan Oomph! I forgot to duck.

Narrator The real workout starts.

Dan Tae kwon do is unarmed combat. You can't beat us.

Mia It's more than that. The instructor said that it's a way of life and thinking.

Dan   Huh?

Holly   Tae kwon do makes your mind
and body strong.

Dan   If my body was any stronger
it would be used as a weapon.

Jake   No one's come here to think.
They've come to fight.

Ethan   I think he's right.

Narrator By the end of the day
they are tired but on a high.

Dan   Did you see what I did to Jake?
We kept eye contact.
But when he attacked I was too fast.
I did a jumping front kick,
then a spinning hook kick.

Ethan   Did he?

Jake   Yeah, I've got the bruises to show it.

Ethan   The instructor was amazing, wasn't he?
You got to feel the force of each block,
punch and kick.

Dan   Guys, watch this. I can fling one leg
up high and push away from the floor
with the other. It's like flying.

Ethan   I used an elbow strike
on the wooden blocks.

Dan   Did they break?

Ethan   No, but I've got bruises on my bruises.

Narrator   The girls are not impressed
by all the macho show and tell.

Mia   My favourite bit was doing the series
of steps.

Holly   I loved forming patterns.

Dan   What are you on about?
Patterns have nothing to do with it.

Holly   Hello! You've been doing
              them all afternoon.

Ethan   Patterns. Like in sewing and knitting?

Holly   Don't you guys know anything?
              Each time you defend and attack
              you do it in a set pattern.

Jake   Of course we know that, don't we?

Dan   Yeah.

Ethan   Sure.

Mia   I love it when the patterns work perfectly.

Jake   I love the yelling.

Dan   Yeah, me too.
And the fighting.

Mia   I've had enough of this.

Holly   Me too. Let's go.

Scene 4
Enter the ninja

Narrator The next day starts with a warm-up run. Jake arrives late.

Ethan Check out Jake. He's wearing a headband with 'ninja' on it.

Dan No way!

Holly Is he for real?

Mia Um, Jake? Didn't ninja spies sneak into enemy camps and houses?

Jake Yeah, they did. They wore masks to hide who they were.

Mia   So wouldn't wearing a headband
with 'ninja' on it be a bit of a giveaway?

Jake   Ah, yes, you could think that.

Narrator They spend two hours learning judo,
then stop for a break.

Jake   Phew! I'm sweaty.
Take a whiff.

Dan   Sweat's good.
It means you've had a hard workout.

Ethan   My feet stink.
I didn't know bare feet could stink.

Mia   Believe me, they can.
I can smell them from here.

Jake   Did you see my blisters?

Ethan   No. I was too busy picking myself
up off the ground.
Show me.

Dan   Hey, better still.
Go and show Holly.

Holly   Don't you dare!

Narrator   Jake does a sidekick that brings
his foot right by Holly's face.

Holly   Gross! I'm out of here.

Mia   Me too.

Narrator   The girls walk off.

Ethan   What's up with them?
They look angry.

Jake   I dunno.

Dan   Must have been something you said!

Jake   I guess.

Ethan   Now what will we do?

Jake   About what?

Ethan   The demo to see which team's best.

Dan   Oh, that.

Jake   We must win. The prize is movie tickets to see *Eager Ninjas part 5*.

Dan   Of course we'll win. I'm here.

Narrator Ethan gulps down a sports drink
too quickly. He splutters and coughs.

Ethan But you can't do that fancy girly
footwork.

Dan The other team's all guys.
I bet they won't be dancing about.

Jake Nah, but they look good.
We need Holly and Mia.

Ethan You'll go and say you're sorry then?

Dan Let's just say we'll get them back.

Narrator Dan has a quick word with Jake.
Jake grins and nods.
They catch up with the girls.

Holly What do you want?

Dan It's Ethan, he's really upset
that you left.

Mia So?

Jake   No kidding. He's been crying.

Holly   Yeah, sure.

Dan   See for yourself.

Narrator   The girls walk back inside.
Ethan's eyes are red and watery
from the coughing.

Holly   We'll talk to him.

Jake   No!

Dan   Jake means Ethan will be really
embarrassed if he knows we told you.

Holly   All right, we'll come back.

Mia   And this has nothing to do
with the demo?

Narrator Dan looks around the hall.
He acts surprised to see the instructors
setting up stations.

Dan Oh, that! We'd forgotten,
hadn't we Jake?

Jake Yeah, what with Ethan being so upset.

Mia I bet.

Narrator Both teams meet their opponents.
They shake hands and bow
to each other before starting.
Mia, Dan and Ethan go
to their stations.

Jake This isn't fair. Mia's way smaller
than the guy she's up against.

Holly Wait! She's got him off balance.
She's moved back and he's falling.
And he's smacked his head on the mat.
She's won!

Narrator Mia walks over to join Holly and Jake.

Mia That was fun.
How are the others doing?

Holly Dan flipped his guy onto his stomach.
They struggled and rolled over.
Now Dan's on his back and he could be
in trouble.

Jake Ethan's doing okay with kick-boxing.
He did a left elbow and right knee
combo.

Holly Yeah, but so did the other guy.

Narrator Dan grabs his opponent's top
and pulls it around his throat.

Jake Hey Dan, should his face
be turning purple?

Mia The guy's struggling.
Now he's tapping out and giving up.

Narrator Dan releases him with a big
winner's smile. Ethan also finishes
and comes over.

Dan Did you win?

Ethan Hard to tell.

Dan Okay ninja Jake, do your stuff.

Narrator Jake yells and circles his arms
above his head like a helicopter.
He runs at his opponent.

Holly What's he doing?

Ethan It's his secret ninja trick.

Dan Hey! He got the guy right in the side
of his face.

Mia   Jake! That was a full speed strike.

Jake   Yeah, good wasn't it?
The instructors said the teams are level.

Ethan   It's up to you Holly.
If you win, we all do.

Narrator The instructors help the boxers
with their gear. The sparring begins.

Jake   Remember to duck, Holly.

Ethan   And weave.

Dan   And sway like a cobra.
Wow! She got him.

Narrator   They all cheer.

Dan   We won!

Mia   Well done, Holly.

Ethan   Yeah, we won!

Dan   See, I told you guys that girls
            can do martial arts.

Drama ideas

After Scene 1

- With a partner, pretend to be Dan and Jake.
- What do they think of Mia and Holly? How are they going to behave towards the girls the next day? Act out a short discussion between them.

After Scene 2

- In your group, each choose a character from the play. Imagine the character's thoughts at the end of the scene.
- Take on the role of your character, and tell the rest of the group what you are thinking.

After Scene 3

- Hotseating: Choose one person to be Jake, and another person to be Mia.

- Everyone else can take turns asking them both the same question, e.g. "What do you like best about martial arts?" They will probably give very different answers!

After Scene 4

- In your group, think together about what could happen next, now that the boys and the girls have won the competition together.

- Act out your ideas.